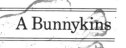

A Bunnykins

Nursery Rhymes

Illustrated by Colin Twinn

Ring-a-ring o' roses

Ring-a-ring o' roses,
A pocket full of posies,
A-tishoo! A-tishoo!
We all fall down.

The cows are in the meadow,
Eating all the grass,
A-tishoo! A-tishoo!
Who's up last?

The grand old Duke of York

O, the grand old Duke of York,
He had ten thousand men;
He marched them up to the top of the hill
And he marched them down again.
And when they were up they were up,
And when they were down they were down,

And when they were only halfway up
They were neither up nor down.

Mary, Mary

'Mary, Mary, quite contrary,
How does your garden grow?'
'With silver bells and cockle shells,
and pretty maids all in a row.'

Sing a song of sixpence

Sing a song of sixpence,
A pocket full of rye.
Four and twenty blackbirds
Baked in a pie.

When the pie was opened
The birds began to sing.
Wasn't that a dainty dish
To set before a king?

The king was in his counting house,
Counting out his money;
The queen was in the parlour,
Eating bread and honey.

The maid was in the garden,
Hanging out the clothes,
When down came a blackbird
And pecked off her nose.

Little Miss Muffet

Little Miss Muffet
Sat on her tuffet,
Eating her curds and whey,
There came a big spider,
Who sat down beside her
And frightened Miss Muffet
away.

Jack and Jill

Jack and Jill went up the hill
To fetch a pail of water.
Jack fell down and broke his crown
And Jill came tumbling after.

Up Jack got, and home did trot,
As fast as he could caper.
Went to bed to mend his head
With vinegar and brown paper.

Old King Cole

Old King Cole was a merry old soul,
And a merry old soul was he.
He called for his pipe,
And he called for his bowl,
And he called for his fiddlers three.

Every fiddler had a very fine
fiddle,
And a very fine fiddle had he.
O, there's none so rare
As can compare
With King Cole and his fiddlers
three.

Polly, put the kettle on

Polly, put the kettle on,
Polly, put the kettle on,
Polly, put the kettle on,
We'll all have tea.

Sukey, take it off again,
Sukey, take it off again,
Sukey, take it off again,
They've all gone away.

Wee Willie Winkie

Wee Willie Winkie runs through the town,
Upstairs and downstairs, in his nightgown.
Rapping at the window and crying through
                                    the lock,
'Are all the children in their beds; it's past
                                eight o'clock?'

FREDERICK WARNE

Published by the Penguin Group
27 Wrights Lane, London W8 5TZ, England
Viking Penguin Inc., 40 West 23rd Street, New York, New York 10010, USA
Penguin Books Australia Ltd, Ringwood, Victoria, Australia
Penguin Books Canada Ltd, 2801 John Street, Markham, Ontario, Canada L3R 1B4
Penguin Books (NZ) Ltd, 182–190 Wairau Road, Auckland 10, New Zealand

Penguin Books Ltd, Registered Offices: Harmondsworth, Middlesex, England

First published 1988
3 5 7 9 10 8 6 4 2
Copyright © Frederick Warne & Co., 1988
Illustrations copyright © 1988 Royal Doulton
Bunnykins ® is a registered trademark of Royal Doulton

ISBN 0 7232 3563 5

Printed and bound in Great Britain by
William Clowes Limited, Beccles and London